My a Book

by Jane Belk Moncure
illustrated by Pam Peltier

Library of Congress Cataloging in Publication Data

Moncure, Jane Belk.
  My "a" book.

  (My first steps to reading)
  Rev. ed. of: My "a" sound box. © 1984.
  Summary: Little a fills his box with things beginning
with the letter "a" and is treated to a ride by an
astronaut.
  1. Children's stories, American. [1. Alphabet]
I. Peltier, Pam, ill. II. Moncure, Jane Belk. My
"a" sound box. III. Title. IV. Series: Moncure,
Jane Belk. My first steps to reading.
PZ7.M739My 1984b   [E]   84-17535
ISBN 0-89565-272-2

Distributed by Childrens Press, 5440 North Cumberland Avenue,
Chicago, Illinois 60656

My "a" Book

(This book concentrates on the short "a" sound in the story line. Words beginning with the long "a" sound are included at the end of the book.)

Little  a had a box.

He said, "I will fill my  ."

Little **a** put on his hat and went for a walk.

He found
apples,
apples,
apples.

He put the apples into his box.

Little  found an alligator.

He put the alligator into his box.

Little  found ants,
ants, ants.

"In you go, ants," he said.

Then Little  found arrows,
arrows,
arrows.

14

Did he put the arrows into his box?

He did!

Little **a** found an ax.

It was a toy ax.

He put the ax into the box.

Now the box was so full …

the ants,

the arrows,

and the ax
fell out.

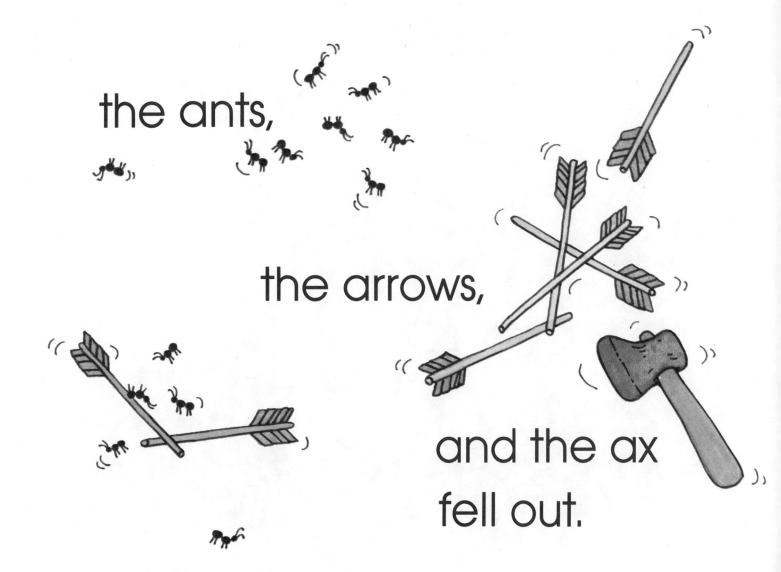

The apples and

the alligator

fell out too.

"Who will help me
fill my box?" said Little a.

An astronaut came by.
"I will help you," said the
astronaut.

"We will fill your box."

Then the astronaut

took Little  for a ride.

25

Up, up, and away!

ants

alligator

arrows

astronaut

apples

ax

More words with Little 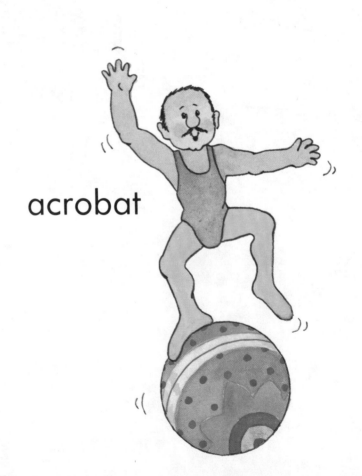a.

antelope

acrobat

antlers

anchor

animals

ambulance

29

Little 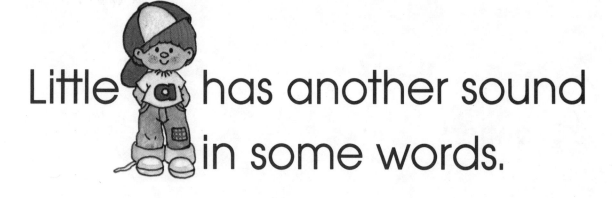 has another sound
in some words.

He says his name.
Listen for Little 's name.

acorn

apron